THE OFFICIAL
Heart of Midlothian
ANNUAL 2017

Written by Sven Houston

Designed by Lucy Boyd

A Grange Publication

© 2016. Published by Grange Communications Ltd., Edinburgh, under licence from Heart of Midlothian Football Club plc. Printed in the EU.

Photographs © SNS Group.

ISBN 978-1-911287-05-6

CONTENTS

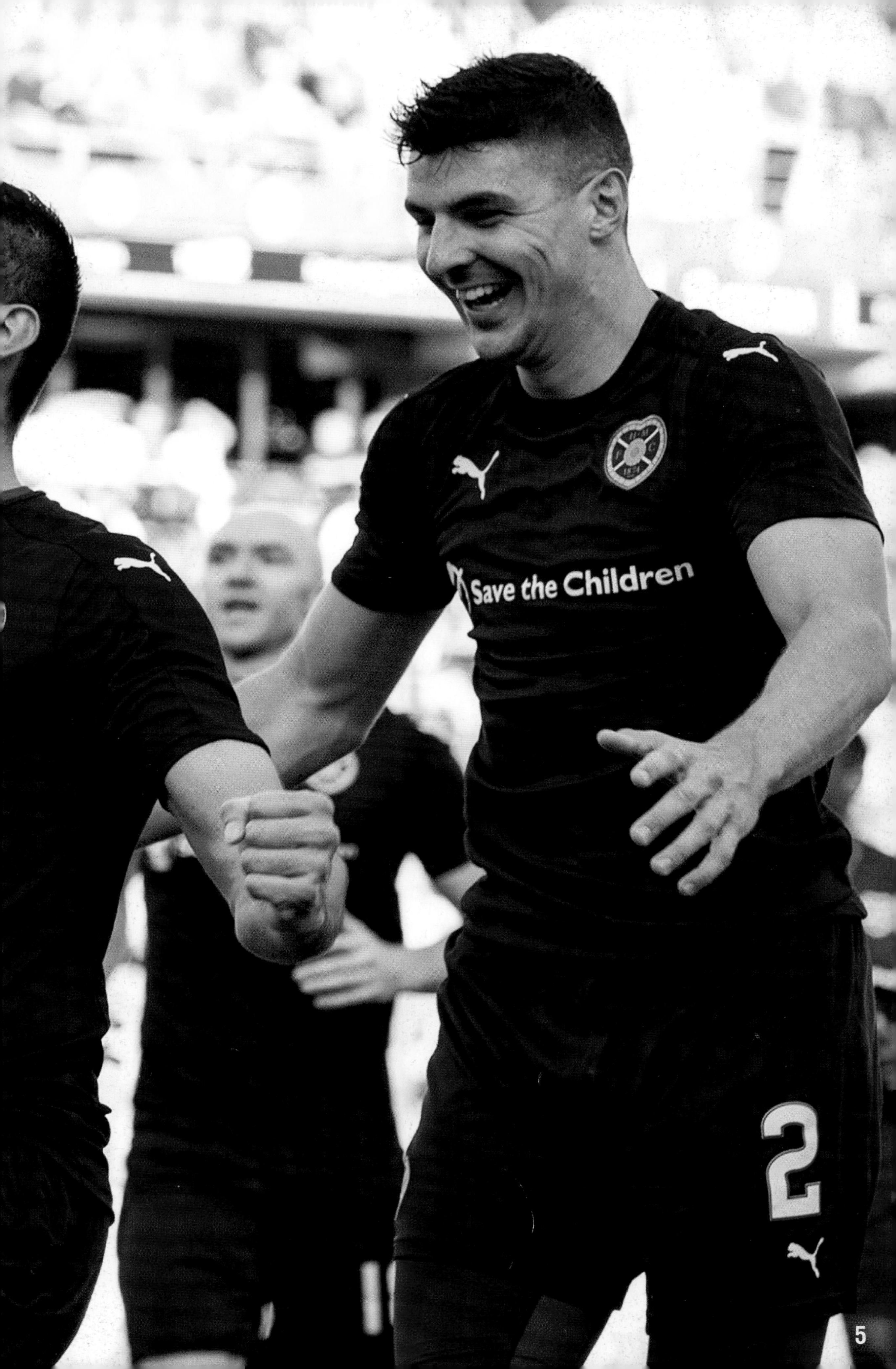
Save the Children

Hello and welcome to the 2017 Heart of Midlothian Annual.

Our first season back in the Ladbrokes Premiership proved to be a great success as we secured third-place and a return to European football.

I was absolutely delighted with how the team responded to the challenge of stepping up to the top-flight and the Season Review pages within this Annual have triggered many fond memories of the 2015/16 campaign.

The success we have enjoyed over the last few seasons wouldn't be possible without you, the supporters. The backing of the Hearts fans has been nothing short of magnificent during my time at the club. I have lost count of the number of home sell-outs we had at Tynecastle last season and I can't stress enough how much it means to the players and I to step out in front of such a passionate support.

Our job is to give you all a team you can have been proud of and we will continue to do our very best to ensure that happens.

Thank you for your incredible support!

Robbie Neilson

Head Coach

CLUB STATS

HONOURS BOARD

Scottish Champions: 1894-95, 1896-97, 1957-58, 1959-60

Runners-Up: 1893-94, 1898-99, 1903-04, 1905-06, 1914-15, 1937-38, 1953-54, 1956-57, 1958-59, 1964-65, 1985-86, 1987-88, 1991-92, 2005-06

Scottish Cup Winners: 1890-91, 1895-96, 1900-01, 1905-06, 1955-56, 1997-98, 2005-06, 2011-12

Scottish Cup Finalists: 1902-03, 1906-07, 1967-68, 1975-76, 1985-86, 1995-96

Scottish League Cup Winners: 1954-55, 1958-59, 1959-60, 1962-63

Scottish League Cup Finalists: 1961-62, 1996-97, 2012-13

First Division Champions: 1979-80

Scottish Championship Winners: 2014-15

First Division Runners-Up: 1977-78, 1982-83

Scottish League East & North Division Runners-Up: 1939-40

Victory Cup Finalists: 1918-19

Scottish Southern League Cup Finalists: 1940-41

Texaco Cup Finalists: 1970-71

FORMED: 1874

COLOURS: Maroon and White

NICKNAME(S): Hearts, The Jam Tarts, Jambos

OWNER: Ann Budge

HEAD COACH: Robbie Neilson

DIRECTOR OF FOOTBALL: Craig Levein

OFFICIAL CLUB WEBSITE: www.heartsfc.co.uk

STADIUM: Tynecastle Stadium

CAPACITY: 17,420 (all seated)

RECORD ATTENDANCE:
53,396 v Rangers (Scottish Cup) February 13, 1932

MOST APPEARANCES: Gary Mackay (640 apps) 1980-97

MOST INTERNATIONAL CAPS:
Steven Pressley (32 Scotland appearances) from 2000-06

BIGGEST VICTORY: 21-0 vs Anchor (Edinburgh FA Cup, 1880)

RECORD LEAGUE APPEARANCES: Gary Mackay (515 apps) 1980-97

RECORD LEAGUE GOALS: John Robertson (214 goals) 1981-98

RECORD LEAGUE GOALS IN A SEASON:
Barney Battles Jr (44 goals) 1930-31

RECORD LEAGUE VICTORY:
10-0 vs Cowdenbeath (28th February 2015)

EUROPEAN RECORD

CHAMPIONS LEAGUE: 4 matches (2006-07)

EUROPEAN CHAMPIONS CUP: 4 matches (1958-59 and 1960-61)

EUROPEAN CUP-WINNERS' CUP: 10 matches (1976-77, 1996-97, 1998-99)

UEFA CUP: 38 matches (1985-86, 1986-87, 1988-89, 1990-91, 1992-93, 1993-94, 2000-01, 2003-04, 2004-05, 2006-07)

UEFA EUROPA LEAGUE: 12 matches (2009-10, 2011-12, 2012-13, 2016-17)

EUROPEAN FAIRS CUP: 12 matches (1961-62, 1963-64, 1965-66)

CENTURY OF EUROPEAN GOALS

Hearts' return to European football in the summer of 2016 saw them surpass a century of goals in Europe. The 100th strike was courtesy of Andrei Kalimullin's own goal in the Jambos' 2-1 1st Round, 1st leg match against FC Infonet.

The total number currently stands at 105. Below is a list of some of the milestone goals throughout the years, starting with the Jambos' first European outing back in 1958.

NO	MATCH	DATE
1	Ian Crawford vs Royal Standard Club Liegeois	Wed 03 Sep 1958
10	Tommy Traynor vs Lausanne	Wed 25 Sep 1963
20	Alan Anderson vs Zaragoza	Wed 12 Jan 1966
30	Drew Busby vs SV Hamburg	Wed 20 Oct 1976
40	Kenny Black vs St Patrick's Athletic	Wed 05 Oct 1988
50	John Robertson vs Dnipro Dnipropetrovsk	Wed 03 Oct 1990
60	John Colquhoun vs Atletico Madrid	Tue 14 Sep 1993
70	Darren Jackson vs IBV-Vestmannaeyjar	Thu 10 Aug 2000
80	Andy Webster vs Braga	Thu 16 Sep 2004
90	Saulius Mikoliunas vs AEK Athens	Wed 09 Aug 2006
100	Andrei Kalimullin (OG) vs FC Infonet Tallinn	Thu 30 Jun 2016

Top Goalscorers (2 goals or more)

7	John Robertson
5	Mike Galloway, Willie Wallace
4	Mark de Vries, Wayne Foster
3	Willie Gibson, Don Kerrigan
2	Alan Anderson, Willie Bauld, Drew Busby, John Colquhoun, Norrie Davidson, Danny Ferguson, Iain Ferguson, Jim Hamilton, Dave McPherson, Igor Rossi, Ryan Stevenson, Tommy Traynor, Andy Webster

SEASON 2015/16 REVIEW

Hearts marked their return to the Scottish top flight in style, culminating in a third place finish which saw the team secure a return to European football.

Any doubts about Hearts' ability to re-adapt to life in the Ladbrokes Premiership were swiftly cast aside as Robbie Neilson's men enjoyed a fantastic first season back in the top division. Here we look back at a number of the key fixtures from a season that ended with European qualification.

AUGUST 2, 2015

Hearts 4 (Juanma, Walker, Paterson, Nicholson)
St Johnstone 3

A sold-out Tynecastle was treated to a seven-goal thriller as the men in maroon beat St Johnstone on the opening day of the season. New boy Juanma wasted little time in introducing himself to the maroon faithful as he fired the Jambos ahead inside four minutes.

Goals from Jamie Walker and Callum Paterson either side of a Simon Lappin strike put Hearts 3-1 up in the second half. The Saints then fought back to make it 3-3 thanks to goals from John Sutton and Graham Cummins.

Hearts were determined to kick-start their season in style, however, and Sam Nicholson sealed the three points with a close-range strike in the 79th minute.

Hearts: Alexander, Paterson, Ozturk, Augustyn, Rossi, Nicholson, Buaben, Gomis, Walker (McGhee, 87), Sow (Reilly, 90), Juanma (McHattie, 77).

AUGUST 8, 2015

Dundee 1
Hearts 2 (Juanma x2)

Following on from their thrilling opening-day victory, Robbie Neilson's men made it two wins out of two courtesy of a Juanma double at Dens Park.

Hearts were made to work hard for the three points, however, as the home side took the lead through Kane Hemmings in a first half they very much dominated.

The Jambos came flying out the traps in the second half and Juanma made it 1-1 from the penalty spot on 56 minutes.

The Spanish target man then grabbed the winning goal three minutes later, breaking free on the left before slotting a low shot beyond the Dundee keeper.

It was an impressive comeback from the Gorgie boys who continued their 100% start to the season.

Hearts: Alexander, Paterson, Augustyn, Rossi, Oshaniwa (King, 75), Ozturk, Buaben, Gomis, Walker, Sow (Nicholson, 53), Juanma (Reilly, 80).

AUGUST 12, 2015

Hearts 2 (Reilly, King)
Motherwell 0

Hearts returned to Tynecastle for the midweek visit of Motherwell and once again proved too strong for the opposition.

Robbie Neilson made three changes to the side that defeated Dundee, with Gavin Reilly, Sam Nicholson and Billy King named in the starting XI.

The changes would prove to be key as Reilly fired the hosts in front from the penalty spot in the first half.

Hearts bossed the game for large periods and were clearly oozing confidence following their impressive start to the season. The game was wrapped up on 64 minutes when King cut in from the right and drilled an unstoppable shot beyond Ripley in the Motherwell goal.

Hearts: Alexander, Paterson, Ozturk, Rossi (McGhee, 84), Oshaniwa, King (Oliver, 88), Buaben, Gomis, Nicholson, Reilly, Sow (Juanma, 59).

AUGUST 15, 2015

Ross County 1
Hearts 2 (Sow, Ozturk)

Hearts' impressive run of form showed no sign of letting up as they journeyed north to Dingwall for a showdown with Ross County.

The Jambos raced into an early two-goal lead thanks to quick-fire strikes from Osman Sow and Alim Ozturk. Liam Boyce pulled one back for The Staggies shortly before half-time, but the boys in maroon held on to seal their fourth straight league victory.

Hearts: Alexander, Paterson, Ozturk, Rossi, Oshaniwa, Sow (Reilly, 57), Buaben (McGhee, 53), Gomis, Nicholson (King, 68), Walker, Juanma.

AUGUST 22, 2015

Hearts 3 (Sow, Nicholson, Juanma)
Partick Thistle 0

Hearts were in a buoyant mood for the visit of Partick Thistle and once again produced a five-star performance in front of a packed Tynecastle.

Gavin Reilly replaced the injured Jamie Walker in the only change from the previous outing, but it was fellow striker Osman Sow who opened the scoring from close range.

The Jambos carried their first-half superiority into the final 45 and Sam Nicholson made it 2-0. Juanma saw his penalty saved, but Sam was quick off the mark to fire home the rebound.

The tie was put to bed just three minutes later when Nicholson found Juanma in space and the Spaniard coolly chipped the keeper to seal a fifth straight win.

Hearts: Alexander, Paterson, Ozturk, Gomis, Buaben (McKirdy, 74), Sow (King, 64), Nicholson, Oshaniwa, Rossi, Juanma (Morrison, 86), Reilly.

SEPTEMBER 23, 2015

Kilmarnock 2
Hearts 3 (Ozturk, Juanma, Nicholson)

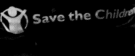

Hearts produced a stunning late comeback at Rugby Park to book a place in the quarter finals of the Scottish League Cup.

Josh Magennis put the hosts ahead early in the first half and it took until the 73rd minute for Hearts to find a leveller, courtesy of skipper Alim Ozturk.

The game burst into life for the final 15 minutes as Magennis scored a second to restore Killie's lead. Just as all looked to be lost, however, Juanma popped up to send a bullet header beyond Jamie MacDonald.

The late equaliser spurred the Jambos on and Sam Nicholson scored in injury time to send the travelling maroon faithful home happy.

Hearts: Alexander, Paterson, Augustyn, Ozturk, Rossi, Buaben, Gomis, Nicholson, Swanson (Juanma, 56), King (Walker, 51), Sow.

SEPTEMBER 26, 2015

Celtic 0
Hearts 0

Following on from their late comeback at Rugby Park, Robbie Neilson's men journeyed to the east end of Glasgow for a showdown with champions Celtic. The Jambos were put under some intense pressure for large periods of the game, but their disciplined performance earned them a credible 0-0 draw at Celtic Park.

The hosts went close on numerous occasions, but the Hearts rearguard held firm throughout. The boys in maroon could well have nicked a goal in the dying seconds when Sam Nicholson broke free, only to be bundled over by Efe Ambrose who was subsequently sent off.

Hearts: Alexander, Paterson, Augustyn, Rossi, Oshaniwa, Gomis, Pallardo, Nicholson, Walker (Djoum, 79), Sow (Buaben, 64), Juanma (Reilly, 76).

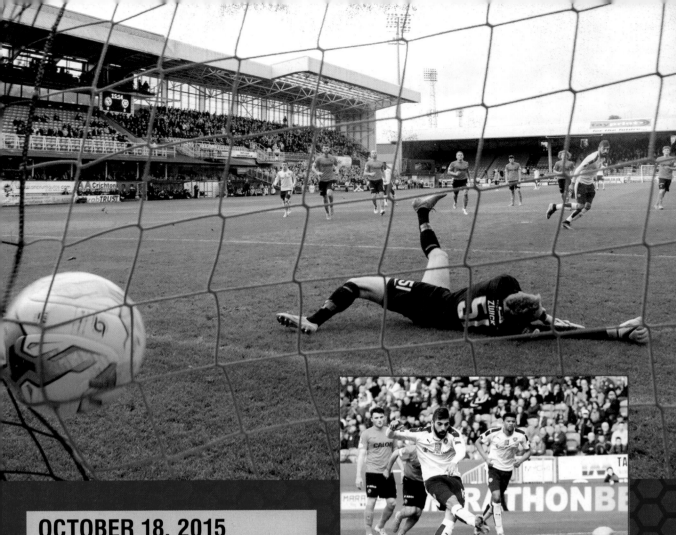

OCTOBER 18, 2015

Dundee United 0
Hearts 1 (Juanma)

Hearts marked their return from the October international break with a fine 1-0 victory over Dundee United.

The only goal of the game came in the 15th minute when Sam Nicholson was taken down by Blair Spittal inside the box. The referee duly pointed to the spot and Juanma stepped up to fire the penalty beyond the keeper.

The hosts ramped up the pressure towards the end of the game, with numerous Hearts players suffering from cramp. The Jambos were in no mood to surrender, however, and held on to seal the three points.

Hearts: Alexander, McGhee, Augustyn, Rossi, Oshaniwa (L. Smith, 69), Buaben, Pallardo (Gomis, 69), Swanson (Walker, 53), Nicholson, Juanma, Sow.

OCTOBER 31, 2015

Partick Thistle 0
Hearts 4 (Juanma x2, Sow x2)

There was to be no Halloween horror show for the Gorgie Boys as doubles from Juanma and Osman Sow helped Hearts sweep Partick aside.

The Jambos took the lead just after the half-hour mark when Juanma got on the end of a Sow cut-back to fire home from close range. The Spaniard then turned provider shortly after the interval as he teed up Sow who made it 2-0.

Juanma grabbed Hearts' third from the penalty spot on 62 minutes, before Sow wrapped up a convincing win with yet another penalty five minutes from time. The goalkeeper, incidentally, was former Hearts attacker Ryan Stevenson who was forced to pull on the gloves following the dismissal of Jags keeper Ryan Scully.

Hearts: Alexander, Paterson, McGhee, Rossi, Oshaniwa, Djoum, Buaben, Nicholson (Zanatta, 70), Swanson (Gomis, 58), Juanma (King, 63), Sow.

Motherwell 2
Hearts 2 (Juanma, Sow)

The Jambos took to the field wearing the Foundation of Hearts tribute jersey for the very first time, but had to settle for a share of the spoils at Fir Park.

The Steelmen went ahead inside two minutes courtesy of Lewis Moult, but Juanma levelled the score eight minutes later with a delightful dink over Conor Ripley.

Marvin Johnson restored Well's lead on 65 minutes, before Sow levelled in spectacular fashion. With no one around him, the Swedish striker unleashed a thunderbolt into the top corner from a good 30 yards out to seal a point for his side.

Hearts: Alexander, Paterson, Augustyn, Rossi, Oshaniwa (McGhee, 50), Pallardo, Djoum, Nicholson, Swanson (Buaben, 68), Juanma, Sow.

DECEMBER 27, 2015

Hearts 2 (Nicholson, Sow)
Celtic 2

Osman Sow produced another stunning strike to rescue a point for Hearts in a thrilling festive fixture at Tynecastle.

The visitors took the lead on 41 minutes through Nir Bitton, but Sam Nicholson equalised minutes later as the two sides headed into the interval on level terms.

Hearts turned up the pressure in the second half but found themselves 2-1 down on 70 minutes when Tom Rogic rifled a shot beyond Alexander.

The three points looked to be heading back to Glasgow until Hearts won a free-kick deep into injury time. Sow stepped up and leathered a 25-yard effort into the top left corner, much to the delight of the Tynecastle faithful.

Hearts: Alexander, Paterson, Augustyn, Rossi, Oshaniwa, Buaben, Gomis (Zanatta, 86), Djoum (Pallardo, 61), Nicholson, Reilly (King, 80), Sow.

JANUARY 9, 2016

Hearts 1 (Paterson)
Aberdeen 0

Having kicked off the New Year with a 2-2 draw at Kilmarnock, Hearts hosted Aberdeen in a Scottish Cup Fourth Round tie under the floodlights in Gorgie.

Tynecastle erupted inside two minutes as Hearts got off to the best possible start. Sam Nicholson's corner from the left found Alim Ozturk who headed the ball towards goal and up popped Callum Paterson to nod the ball into the net.

Hearts produced a stunning display on the night and held on to advance despite some late Dons pressure.

JANUARY 16, 2016

Hearts 6 (Rossi, Sow, Reilly, Paterson, Juanma, Djoum)
Motherwell 0

Buoyed by their Scottish Cup victory over Aberdeen, Hearts ran riot at Tynecastle the following week as they put six past The Steelmen.

Six different players found themselves on the scoresheet as Hearts produced a breathtaking performance in Gorgie. The Jambos were 3-0 up inside 22 minutes courtesy of strikes from Igor Rossi, Osman Sow and a Gavin Reilly penalty.

After a blistering opening 45 minutes, the second-half was a more subdued affair until it burst into life with just over 10 minutes to go.

Substitute Dario Zanatta teed up Callum Paterson for the fourth, before Juanma rifled home the fifth shortly after. Finally, Arnaud Djoum made it six from the penalty spot in the dying minutes.

Hearts: Alexander, Paterson, Ozturk, Augustyn, Rossi (McGhee, 83), Buaben, Pallardo, Djoum, King, Reilly (Zanatta, 69), Sow (Juanma, 64).

FEBRUARY 7, 2016

Hearts 2 (Djoum, Nicholson)
Hibs 2

Despite Hibs plying their trade in the second-tier, Edinburgh was not to be denied a derby in the 2015/16 season as the two rivals were paired together in the Scottish Cup Fifth Round.

The Jambos raced into a two-goal lead at a sold out Tynecastle, with a stunning Arnaud Djoum strike putting the hosts 1-0 up. Sam Nicholson then made it 2-0 before the interval, but a late Hibs comeback saw them earn a replay thanks to goals from Jason Cummings and Paul Hanlon.

Unfortunately, the Jambos succumbed to a 1-0 defeat in the replay at Easter Road.

Hearts: Alexander, Paterson, Ozturk (Oshaniwa, 50), Augustyn, McGhee, Nicholson, Djoum (Walker, 82), Pallardo, Buaben (Cowie, 9), Reilly, Dauda.

FEBRUARY 10, 2016

Ross County 0
Hearts 3 (Walker (OG), Dauda x2)

New boy Abiola Dauda opened his goalscoring account for the Jambos with a brace against Ross County in a midweek encounter in Dingwall.

Robbie Neilson made five changes to the side that played Hibs three days previously, with John Souttar and Jordan McGhee paired in central defence.

The hosts had the majority of play in the first half, but Hearts then grabbed the crucial first goal early in the second half. A Don Cowie corner produced a scramble in the box before the ball eventually crossed the line; Jamie Walker wheeled away in celebration but it was unclear who the ball came off last.

Dauda then came off the bench on the hour mark and sealed the win with two sublime finishes in the 86th and 89th minute.

Hearts: Alexander, Paterson, Souttar, McGhee (L. Smith, 81), Oshaniwa, Cowie, Djoum (Dauda, 61), Pallardo, Nicholson, Walker (Zanatta, 74), Juanma.

APRIL 8, 2016

Hearts 2 (Juanma x2)
Aberdeen 1

Friday night football returned to Gorgie as a Juanma double sealed a memorable victory over Aberdeen under the Tynecastle floodlights.

The second-placed Dons made a dream start as Simon Church opened the scoring inside

four minutes. The visitors threatened to run riot during the opening stages, but Hearts gradually hauled themselves back in the game.

Before long, the home side were dominant and deservedly drew level on 33 minutes when Juanma pounced to fire home a rebound.

The Spaniard then netted the winner in the second-half; Jamie Walker's pin-point cross from the left was met by the striker who sent a bullet header beyond the keeper.

Hearts: Alexander, Souttar, Ozturk, Augustyn, Rossi, Kitchen, Djoum, Buaben (Pallardo, 79), Nicholson, Walker (McGhee, 83), Juanma (Zanatta, 90).

MAY 12, 2016

Aberdeen 0
Hearts 1 (Dauda)

A month later and Hearts faced Aberdeen once again, this time in the penultimate game of the season.

The Jambos had long since secured third spot and a return to European football, but this was nonetheless a closely contested match which was won by a 63rd minute Abiola Dauda strike.

Alim Ozturk's 30-yard free kick was spilled by the 'keeper and Dauda pounced to fire home the rebound; much to the delight of the travelling Jambos.

Hearts:
Hamilton,
Paterson, Ozturk,
Souttar, Oshaniwa,
Zanatta (Nicholson, 67),
Kitchen, Djoum, Buaben,
Juanma (McGhee, 90),
Dauda (Reilly, 78).

MAY 15, 2016

Hearts 2 (Djoum, Shaughnessy (OG))
St Johnstone 2

The Jambos wrapped up a memorable first season back in the Ladbrokes Premiership with a 2-2 draw at home to St Johnstone.

The visitors looked set to spoil the European party as strikes from Liam Craig and Adam Cummins put them 2-0 up inside 12 minutes.

The Jambos were in no mood to lie down, however, as Arnaud Djoum pulled one back on 17 minutes. Three minutes later, Hearts were level as Buaben's cross came off Shaughnessy and into the net.

There were to be no further goals, but the Jambos took to the field post-match to thank the fans for their tremendous support

throughout the campaign. The t-shirts said it all: 'So make some noise, The Gorgie Boys are going to Europe!'

Hearts: Hamilton, Paterson, Ozturk, Souttar, Oshaniwa (L. Smith, 52), Moore (Nicholson, 62), Kitchen, Buaben, Djoum, Juanma (Reilly, 67), Dauda.

DATE	OPPOSITION	SCORE	SCORERS	ATTENDANCE
30 Jul	Arbroath (H) (LC)	4-2	McGhee, Sow (2), Walker	6,240
2 Aug	St Johnstone (H)	4-3	Juanma, Walker, Paterson, Nicholson	16,334
8 Aug	Dundee (A)	1-2	Juanma (2)	8,222
12 Aug	Motherwell (H)	2-0	Reilly, King	16,645
15 Aug	Ross County (A)	1-2	Sow, Ozturk	4,806
22 Aug	Partick Thistle (H)	3-0	Sow, Nicholson, Juanma	16,657
25 Aug	Forfar (A) (League Cup)	1-2 (AET)	McHattie, Reilly	1,844
29 Aug	Hamilton (A)	3-2	King, Paterson	4,745
11 Sep	Inverness CT (A)	2-0		4,160
20 Sep	Aberdeen (H)	1-3	Rossi	16,702
23 Sep	Kilmarnock (A) (LC)	2-3 (AET)	Ozturk, Juanma, Nicholson	3,249
26 Sep	Celtic (A)	0-0		46,297
3 Oct	Kilmarnock (H)	1-1	Walker	16,461
18 Oct	Dundee Utd (A)	0-1	Juanma	7,461
24 Oct	Ross County (H)	2-0	Paterson, Sow	16,264
28 Oct	Celtic (H) (LC)	1-2	Djoum	11,598
31 Oct	Partick (A)	0-4	Juanma (2), Sow (2)	4,776
7 Nov	Hamilton (H)	2-0	Buaben, Djoum	16,121
21 Nov	Dundee (H)	1-1	Djoum	16,736
28 Nov	Motherwell (A)	2-2	Juanma, Sow	5,141
12 Dec	Aberdeen (A)	1-0		13,310
19 Dec	St Johnstone (A)	0-0		4,780

DATE	OPPOSITION	SCORE	SCORERS	ATTENDANCE
27 Dec	Celtic (H)	2-2	Nicholson, Sow	16,844
30 Dec	Dundee Utd (H)	3-2	Reilly, Buaben, Sow	16,721
2 Jan	Kilmarnock (A)	2-2	Reilly, Paterson	5,388
9 Jan	Aberdeen (H) (SC)	1-0	Paterson	13,595
16 Jan	Motherwell (H)	6-0	Rossi, Sow, Reilly, Paterson, Juanma, Djoum	16,574
24 Jan	Hamilton (A)	0-0		2,684
7 Feb	Hibs (H) (SC)	2-2	Djoum, Nicholson	16,846
10 Feb	Ross County (A)	0-3	Walker/OG, Dauda (2)	3,391
16 Feb	Hibs (A) (SC Replay)	1-0		19,433
20 Feb	Dundee Utd (A)	2-1	Walker	8,031
27 Feb	Kilmarnock (H)	1-0	Walker	16,354
1 Mar	Inverness CT (H)	2-0	Walker, Dauda	15,767
5 Mar	Partick (H)	1-0	Djoum	16,558
12 Mar	Dundee (A)	0-1	Walker	6,195
19 Mar	St Johnstone (H)	0-3		16,295
2 Apr	Celtic (A)	3-1	Walker	49,009
8 Apr	Aberdeen (H)	2-1	Juanma (2)	16,995
12 Apr	Inverness CT (A)	0-0		3,202
23 Apr	Motherwell (A)	1-0		5,125
30 Apr	Celtic (H)	1-3	Dauda	16,527
7 May	Ross County (H)	1-1	Juanma	15,438
12 May	Aberdeen (A)	0-1	Dauda	10,087
15 May	St Johnstone (H)	2-2	Djoum, Shaughnessy (OG)	16,046

PLAYER PROFILES

JACK HAMILTON

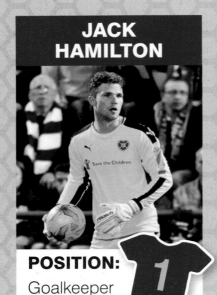

POSITION:
Goalkeeper

BORN:
22/03/94

NATIONALITY:
Scottish

1

CALLUM PATERSON

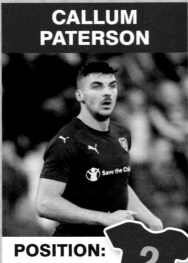

POSITION:
Defender

BORN:
13/10/94

NATIONALITY:
Scottish

2

FAYCAL RHERRAS

POSITION:
Defender

BORN:
07/04/93

NATIONALITY:
Moroccan

3

IGOR ROSSI

POSITION:
Defender

BORN:
10/03/89

NATIONALITY:
Brazilian

4

ALIM OZTURK

POSITION:
Defender

BORN:
17/11/92

NATIONALITY:
Dutch

5

PLAYER PROFILES

PERRY KITCHEN

POSITION:
Midfielder

6

BORN:
29/02/92

NATIONALITY:
American

JAMIE WALKER

POSITION:
Midfielder

7

BORN:
25/06/93

NATIONALITY:
Scottish

PRINCE BUABEN

POSITION:
Midfielder

8

BORN:
23/04/88

NATIONALITY:
Ghanaian

ARNAUD DJOUM

POSITION:
Midfielder

10

BORN:
02/05/89

NATIONALITY:
Cameroon

SAM NICHOLSON

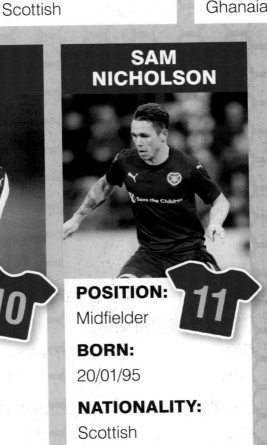

POSITION:
Midfielder

11

BORN:
20/01/95

NATIONALITY:
Scottish

31

PLAYER PROFILES

VIKTOR NORING

POSITION: 13
Goalkeeper

BORN:
03/02/91

NATIONALITY:
Swedish

JOHN SOUTTAR

POSITION: 14
Defender

BORN:
25/09/96

NATIONALITY:
Scottish

DON COWIE

POSITION: 15
Midfielder

BORN:
15/02/83

NATIONALITY:
Scottish

JUWON OSHANIWA

POSITION: 17
Defender

BORN:
14/09/90

NATIONALITY:
Nigerian

CONOR SAMMON

POSITION: 18
Striker

BORN:
06/11/86

NATIONALITY:
Irish

KRYSTIAN NOWAK

POSITION: 19
Defender

BORN:
01/04/94

NATIONALITY:
Polish

PLAYER PROFILES

BJORN JOHNSEN

POSITION: 20
Striker

BORN:
06/11/91

NATIONALITY:
American

ROBBIE MUIRHEAD

POSITION: 23
Striker

BORN:
08/03/96

NATIONALITY:
Scottish

LIAM SMITH

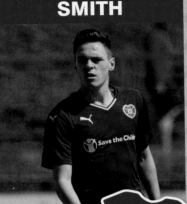

POSITION: 24
Defender

BORN:
10/04/96

NATIONALITY:
Scottish

NIKOLAY TODOROV

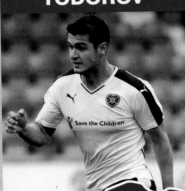

POSITION: 25
Striker

BORN:
24/08/96

NATIONALITY:
Bulgarian

DARIO ZANATTA

POSITION: 26
Midfielder

BORN:
24/05/97

NATIONALITY:
Canadian

TONY WATT

POSITION: 32
Striker

BORN:
29/12/93

NATIONALITY:
Scottish

HEY ARNAUD

Midfield ace Arnaud Djoum is here to stay.

Arnaud Djoum arrived a month into the 2015/16 season, but wasted little time impressing the Gorgie faithful.

The Belgian midfielder made his debut as a substitute in the 0-0 draw at Celtic Park on September 26th. His first start came in a 2-0 home win over Ross County which was soon followed by his first goal in a 2-1 League Cup defeat to Celtic.

Arnaud quickly established himself as a key player and his surging runs and goal threat made him an instant hit with the Hearts support. He made a total of 30 appearances last season, bagging seven goals in the process.

Indeed, his goals at Tynecastle always proved a highlight with fans thanks to stadium announcer Scott Wilson's decision to give him his own goal celebration song – DJ Jazzy Jeff & The Fresh Prince's *Boom! Shake the Room*.

The love from the stands helped him settle quickly and is one of the key reasons behind his decision to sign a new three-year deal in the summer of 2016.

"To know that my long-term future lies here makes me happy. This is a good club for me and it gives me stability," Arnaud explained.

"I see a lot of potential in this team and the club in general. Over the next few years I believe we can only get better, so it's something I really want to be part of.

"It's always a challenge coming to a new club, a risk in many ways because you don't know what to expect.

"But within a few weeks of being here, I knew this was a club for me. I felt at home straight away and made a good connection with my team-mates and the coaches.

"Another big aspect, of course, is the fans. When you play at Tynecastle it is amazing, there is so much noise and the support is great. I've never experienced so much backing from the fans before so it is very good.

"So I have to say thank you to the fans for welcoming me. They helped make it an easy decision to commit my future to this club."

One goal in particular stands out from the 2015/16 campaign; his stunning strike against city rivals Hibs.

"I have many happy memories from last season," he said. "I think my best moment was scoring against Hibs in the Cup. I know it didn't end well, but it was still an incredible feeling to score in a derby at Tynecastle.

"Obviously finishing in third place was another great achievement for me and the team.

"But we have to look to improve every year. We have a good squad here, we are all in this together and we are hungry for success."

Answers on p.60-61

QUIZ

1 Which position did Hearts finish in last season?

3rd.

2 In what year did Hearts first win the Scottish Cup?

1800

3 What shirt number does Conor Sammon wear?

18

4 Who is Hearts' all-time league top scorer?

John Robertson

5 Who did Hearts play in this season's first league game?

Celtic

6 What was Hearts' biggest league win last season?

~~Aberdeen~~ Motherwell

7 What nationality is Perry Kitchen?

USa

8 Who did Hearts play in the first round of this season's Europa League?

~~Carl Paterson~~ Ed infonet

9 Which Hearts player made his 100th competitive appearance for the club in the final game of last season?

Sam Nicholson

10 Who was voted last season's Fans' Player of the Year?

DJoum

FAYCAL RHERRAS

WORDSEARCH

Can you find the Hearts words in the grid?

K	D	E	N	O	S	R	E	T	A	P
H	P	L	R	L	H	X	C	A	T	K
A	A	T	M	H	K	X	M	K	B	W
M	T	S	W	M	E	N	Y	J	P	R
I	T	A	K	Y	A	R	A	H	A	L
L	A	C	X	U	N	M	R	T	G	W
T	N	E	J	R	B	E	T	A	Q	R
O	A	N	B	O	Y	U	B	C	S	T
N	Z	Y	S	T	O	M	G	A	T	H
T	M	T	T	S	L	R	R	R	L	U	N
W	A	L	K	E	R	R	G	T	T	B

BUABEN
HAMILTON
JAMBOS
JUANMA
PATERSON

RHERRAS
SOUTTAR
TYNECASTLE
WALKER
ZANATTA

Answers on p.60-61

GUESS WHO?

Can you guess which Hearts players are in the pictures below?

Answers on p.60-61

CONOR SAMMON

SEASON IN NUMBERS

3 Hearts' league finish in the 2015/16 Ladbrokes Premiership. The Jambos enjoyed a fantastic first season back in the top-flight and capped it off by sealing a return to European football.

THANK YOU FOR YOUR INCREDIBLE SUPPORT

16,423 Average home league attendance at Tynecastle.

6-0 Biggest victory of the season as Hearts put six past Motherwell, courtesy of six different scorers: Rossi, Sow, Reilly, Paterson, Juanma, Djoum.

72 Hearts goals in all competitions.

13 The number of goals scored by Hearts top scorer – Juanma. The Spaniard opened his goal scoring account on his home debut against St Johnstone. Another 12 goals followed, including a memorable double in a 2-1 win over Aberdeen.

22 The number of Hearts wins, including 18 league victories, three League Cup wins and one Scottish Cup victory.

GORGIE RULES!

AWARDS

Players, staff and supporters of Heart of Midlothian gathered to celebrate at the club's 2015/16 Player of the Year Awards dinner at the EICC back in April.

The glitzy occasion was enjoyed by around 800 people, with a host of big winners on the night. Host, and the voice of Hearts, Scott Wilson picked up the evening's first award, the Doc Melvin Memorial Award for services to the club.

A Celebration of Youth saw Daniel Baur and Dario Zanatta pick up the U17s and U20s Player of the Year Awards respectively, while Sam Nicholson was crowned the Overall Young Player of the Year, voted for by his team-mates.

Liam Fox was voted Coach of the Year by his peers at the Football Academy in what was a brand new award.

Club stalwart Clare Cowan received the George Nicolson Recognition Award, which recognises an outstanding contribution by an individual at the Hearts Football Academy.

Arnaud Djoum was a double winner, landing the Fans' Player of the Year and Goal of the Season for his stunning strike in the Scottish Cup against Hibs.

Memorable Moment, voted for by the fans, was the last-minute equaliser against Celtic. Sam collected on behalf to the team before the room was treated to a video message all the way from China, courtesy of Osman Sow and Ryan McGowan.

Neil Alexander was given a Special Recognition Award and the Players' Player of the Year was Igor Rossi.

ONES TO WATCH

Marcus Godinho

Marcus joined Hearts in the summer of 2016, having previously played youth football in his native Canada. He spent time with the Toronto FC Academy and has also made numerous appearances for Canada at youth level. The 19-year-old's favoured position is right-back, but his strong technical ability means he can also be deployed in midfield.

Daniel Baur

The 17-year-old towering defender signed a full-time deal with Hearts in 2015. Initially earmarked for the U17 side, he soon found himself heavily involved with Jon Daly's U20 development squad. He played a key role in the Wee Jambos' run to last season's Scottish Youth Cup Final. His aerial prowess is matched by his ability to carry the ball out of defence and his performances last season saw him voted the U17s Player of the Year.

Alex Petkov

The 16-year-old Bulgarian signed for Hearts in the summer of 2016, having been on the club's radar for a considerable amount of time. The technically gifted midfielder will be looking to make his mark with both the Hearts U17s and U20s this season. He is highly regarded within the Hearts Academy and it is hoped he will make the step up to the senior team within the next few years.

Callumn Morrison

The 17-year-old attacker is another young star who has been quick to make his mark in the Hearts U20s side. Much like Daniel Baur, he was instrumental in Hearts' Youth Cup run last season and he contributes with a regular supply of goals and assists. His performances last season caught the eye of coach Robbie Neilson and Callum appearances for the first team.

SUPER DARIO

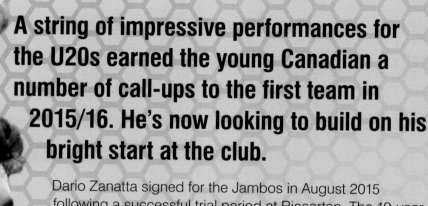

A string of impressive performances for the U20s earned the young Canadian a number of call-ups to the first team in 2015/16. He's now looking to build on his bright start at the club.

Dario Zanatta signed for the Jambos in August 2015 following a successful trial period at Riccarton. The 19-year-old was originally earmarked for the U20 development squad, but soon found himself heavily involved with the first team.

The winger is known for his pace, technique and good finishing, skills which enabled him to flourish in U20s matches. He racked up goals and assists for fun and played a key role in the Wee Jambos' run to the Scottish Youth Cup Final. His efforts saw him voted U20s Player of the Year at the end of the season.

"The Youth Cup was a good experience for us. Of course, we'd have liked the final to have ended differently but we think the experience will stand us in good stead," Dario explained.

"Playing well for the U20s enabled me to get a shot with the first team. It's important to perform every time you step on to the pitch and I'll have to keep doing that going forward.

"To get the U20 Player of the Year Award was a huge honour and will only inspire me to get even better.

"Last season overall was really enjoyable for me and a bit of a whirlwind!

"I came to the club at the start of the season and was lucky enough to get a few first-team opportunities.

"My goal is to get more chances this season. We've got a long track record here at Hearts of bringing players through, just look at Nicholson and Paterson and those guys. So I'm hopeful I'll be the next to step up."

With a number of senior appearances to his name already, few people would bet against the youngster becoming a key member of the Hearts squad within the next few years. If that were to be the case, then his decision to leave Canada as a teenager would prove to be a wise one.

Born in the Western province of British Columbia, Dario spent his formative years within the Vancouver Whitecaps academy system. Such was his drive and ambition, however, that he decided to pack his bags and try his luck in Europe.

Trials with Ipswich and IFK Gothenburg soon followed, but once he arrived in Gorgie he never looked back.

"I felt at home here straight away, it's a really good place for a youngster to play football. I knew this was the right club for me and I've not regretted coming here, that's for sure."

Originally the only Canuck at the club, Dario found himself joined by fellow-countrymen Harry Paton and Marcus Godinho before the start of the 2016/17 season.

"Getting Harry and Marcus in has been great," he said. "I knew of them from before and I've played with them a bit in Canada, so to have them join us here is great. Plus they're great players so that helps."

Could we have a Canadian trio in the Hearts first team before too long? Only time will tell!

LITTLE BIG SHOT YOUTH CUP FINAL

Hearts' U20 side enjoyed a memorable run to the Little Big Shot Youth Cup Final at Hampden last season.

Jon Daly's Wee Jambos defeated East Stirlingshire, Inverness CT and Dundee United en route to the final against Motherwell.

A crowd of nearly 3,000 turned out at the national stadium to watch a highly entertaining game that ultimately ended in disappointment for the young Jambos.

Despite fine strikes from Jordan McGhee and Dario Zanatta, the Steelmen proved too much for the Riccarton lads and eventually emerged 5-2 winners on the night.

The defeat aside, the young Hearts stars could take great pride in their cup run and the experience of featuring in such a prestigious game will stand them in good stead.

MAZE

ck the Jambo is ready and
iting for you to join him at
necastle. Can you find the route
at takes you to the stadium?

TYNECASTLE STADIUM

Answers on
p.60-61

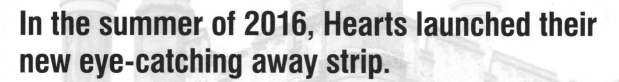

In the summer of 2016, Hearts launched their new eye-catching away strip.

In a radical departure from the traditional maroon of the home strip, the club launched a kit in the colours of primrose yellow and rose pink.

ItIt is a homage to the colours of the 5th Early of Rosebery, a former Honorary President of the Scottish Football Association. He was a keen racehorse owner whose racing colours were primrose yellow and rose pink.

The Scottish national team wore a shirt consisting of those colours on several occasions, most notably in a 6-1 victory over England in 1881. It remains the highest margin of home defeat for England to this day.

Hearts legend Bobby Walker played in the colours from 1900 and his original jersey now takes pride of place in the new Hearts Museum.

The Rosebery Challenge Cup, pictured with Alim Ozturk below, was presented to the winners of an end-of-season competition that lasted from 1882-83 to 1944-45. Hearts won it on 32 occasions.

GETTING TO KNOW...
JOHN SOUTTAR

Position: Central Defender

Signed from: Dundee United (1st Feb 2016)

ON THE PITCH...

WHICH PLAYER WAS YOUR ROLE MODEL GROWING UP?
(Laughs) That has to be Don Cowie! What a guy!

BEST MEMORY AS A HEARTS PLAYER?
I've not been here too long but it'll probably have to be my debut match.

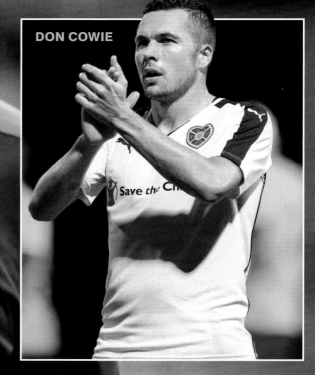

DON COWIE

OFF THE PITCH...

RUMOUR HAS IT YOU'RE A DAB HAND IN THE KITCHEN. WHAT'S YOUR SIGNATURE DISH?
Venison meatballs is my favourite. Complete with a bit of Italian seasoning of course.

FAVOURITE TV SHOW?
Has to be Modern Family.

WHO'S THE BIGGEST CELEBRITY YOU'VE EVER MET?
I've not had many celeb encounters. Perhaps Paddy McGuinness, the chap from Take Me Out. I met him on holiday once. He was alright.

PERSON YOU'D MOST LIKE TO MEET?
Tough one. I'd probably say Phil Dunphy, the character from Modern Family!

TEAM-MATES...

WHO'S THE BIGGEST MOANER?
That would be Callum Paterson. Gav Reilly once said Callum could moan about moaning, so that says it all really.

WHO'S THE EASIEST PLAYER TO WIND UP IN THE DRESSING ROOM?
Jack Hamilton, hands down.

WHO IS THE TOUGHEST OPPONENT YOU'VE PLAYED AGAINST?
That would be Chuba Akpom, the Arsenal striker. I came up against him a few years ago at youth level with Scotland, he's a great player.

AND WORST DRESSER?
Again, that would be Jack Hamilton. He's got this one tracksuit he always wears, it's pretty shocking to be honest.

WHO IS YOUR ROOM MATE ON OVERNIGHT TEAM TRIPS?
Sam Nicholson. I actually lived with him for a while as well, he's some guy!

AND WHAT WOULD YOU SAY IS HIS MOST ANNOYING HABIT?
Probably the fact that he's on the phone to his girlfriend 24/7.

CALLUM PATERSON

SAM NICHOLSON

JAMBOS IN EUROPE

Hearts 2 (Buaben, Kalimullin [OG])
FC Infonet 1

1ST ROUND, 1ST LEG

Hearts' reward for their third place finish in the Ladbrokes Premiership was a welcome return of European football to Tynecastle.

The Jambos were paired with Estonian side FC Infonet in the first round of the qualifying stages. The first leg was played at Tynecastle on June 30th, with Hearts running out 2-1 winners in front of an impressive crowd of 14,417.

The visitors silenced the Gorgie faithful on 20 minutes when Jevgeni Harin fired a stunning volley beyond Jack Hamilton. Hearts responded six minutes later, however, when Prince Buaben levelled the score from the penalty spot.

An Andrei Kalimullin own goal then made it 2-1 to the hosts on 35 minutes as Hearts took a one-goal lead to the return leg in Tallinn.

FC Infonet 2
Hearts 4 (Rossi x2, Paterson, Ozturk)

2ND LEG

Robbie Neilson's men journeyed east to the Estonian capital for the second leg, which was played at the national stadium – A. Le Coq Arena.

Any doubts about Hearts' slender lead going into the away leg were quickly cast aside as the Jambos raced into a three-goal lead before half-time.

Paterson put the Gorgie boys ahead on two minutes with a bullet header. Igor Rossi then made it 2-0 soon after with another header following a Jamie Walker corner.

Walker then made his third assist just before half-time as Ozturk scored from close range. The captain then scored an own goal early in the

second-half, but Rossi then essentially put the tie to bed with another finish following a corner.

The hosts pulled another goal back but Hearts held on to secure their place in the second round.

Birkirkara FC 0
Hearts 0

2ND ROUND, 1ST LEG

Next up for Robbie Neilson's men was a trip to Malta to face Birkirkara FC.

The Jambos faced a tricky task in the Maltese heat, with the opponents having taken West Ham United to penalties in the previous season.

Backed by close to 400 travelling Jambos, however, the Gorgie boys coped well in the in the heat as they played out a 0-0 draw at the aptly named Hibernians Stadium.

Hearts dominated possession throughout and could have taken an early lead had Conor Sammon's effort not been ruled out for offside.

Hearts piled on the pressure towards the end but had to make do with a goalless draw to take home to Tynecastle.

Hearts 1 (Sammon)
Birkirkara FC 2

2ND LEG

The return leg ended in bitter disappointment for the Jambos as the visitors sealed a 2-1 victory in Gorgie.

Prince Buaben missed a first-half penalty and Jamie Walker hit the crossbar as Hearts bowed out of Europe.

Birkirkara proved hard to break down and took the lead on 54 minutes through Christian Bubalovic. They then doubled their advantage 13 minutes later when Edward Herrera finished off a well-executed counter attack.

Conor Sammon pulled one back with a close-range header, however, it wasn't to be as Hearts were eliminated from the Europa League.

FOREVER IN OUR HEARTS

The Forever In Our Hearts Memorial Garden officially opened its gates in December 2015 and has already established itself as a key part of Tynecastle.

The Memorial Garden is located between the Wheatfield and Roseburn Stands. Older supporters may remember it as the location where the famous Shed once stood.

A 3D bronze and steel sculpture of the club's iconic crest sits at the heart of the garden. The sculpture is surrounded by seven benches, each dedicated to one of the seven Hearts players who lost their lives in the Great War.

The walls of the garden feature steel, heart-shaped plaques that have been placed there by supporters in memory of loved ones.

In June 2016, the final touch was added to the garden as the magnificent 1914 Memorial Trust Bronze statue was installed. Overlooking the garden, the statue depicts a young soldier in Royal Scots uniform holding a football and a rifle. The wording on the statue simply reads…The Bravest Team.

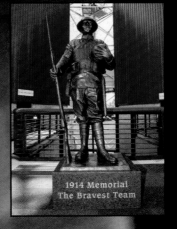

FIVE FACTS ABOUT...
PERRY KITCHEN

Perry was born in Indianapolis, Indiana on February 29th, 1992.

Perry made his Hearts debut as a substitute against Dundee at Dens Park on March 12th 2016.

He has several US international caps to his name & was called up to the 2016 Copa America Squad.

He was selected by D.C. United in the 1st round of the 2011 MLS Superdraft and went on to make 178 appearances for the club.

Perry signed a two-and-a-half-year deal with Hearts on March 9th 2016.

FIVE FACTS ABOUT...
ARNAUD DJOUM

Arnaud Djoum holds a Belgian citizenship but was born in Cameroon.

His formative years were spent with Belgian clubs Brussels and Anderlecht.

His big break came with Dutch side Roda JC, where he made 123 appearances over a five-year period.

Arnaud signed for Hearts in September 2015 following his release from Polish side Lech Poznan.

The fans' favourite scored his first goal for Hearts against Celtic at Tynecastle on October 28th 2015.

QUIZ ANSWERS

Page 36 – Quiz

1. 3rd
2. 1890/91
3. 18
4. John Robertson (214 goals)
5. Celtic
6. 6-0 (vs Motherwell)
7. US
8. FC Infonet
9. Sam Nicholson
10. Arnaud Djoum

Page 38 – Wordsearch

K	D	E	N	O	S	R	E	T	A	P
H	P	L	R	L	H	X	C	A	T	K
A	A	T	M	H	K	X	M	K	B	W
M	T	S	W	M	E	N	Y	J	P	R
I	T	A	K	Y	A	R	A	H	A	L
L	A	C	X	U	N	M	R	T	G	W
T	N	E	J	R	B	E	T	A	Q	R
O	A	N	B	O	Y	U	B	C	S	T
N	Z	Y	S	T	O	M	G	A	T	H
T	M	T	T	S	L	R	R	L	U	N
W	A	L	K	E	R	R	G	T	T	B

Page 39 – Guess Who?

1. **Conor Sammon**
2. **Arnaud Djoum**
3. **Igor Rossi**
4. **Don Cowie**
5. **Jamie Walker**
6. **John Souttar**

Page 50 – Maze

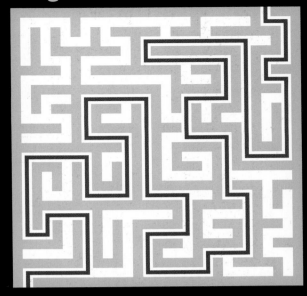

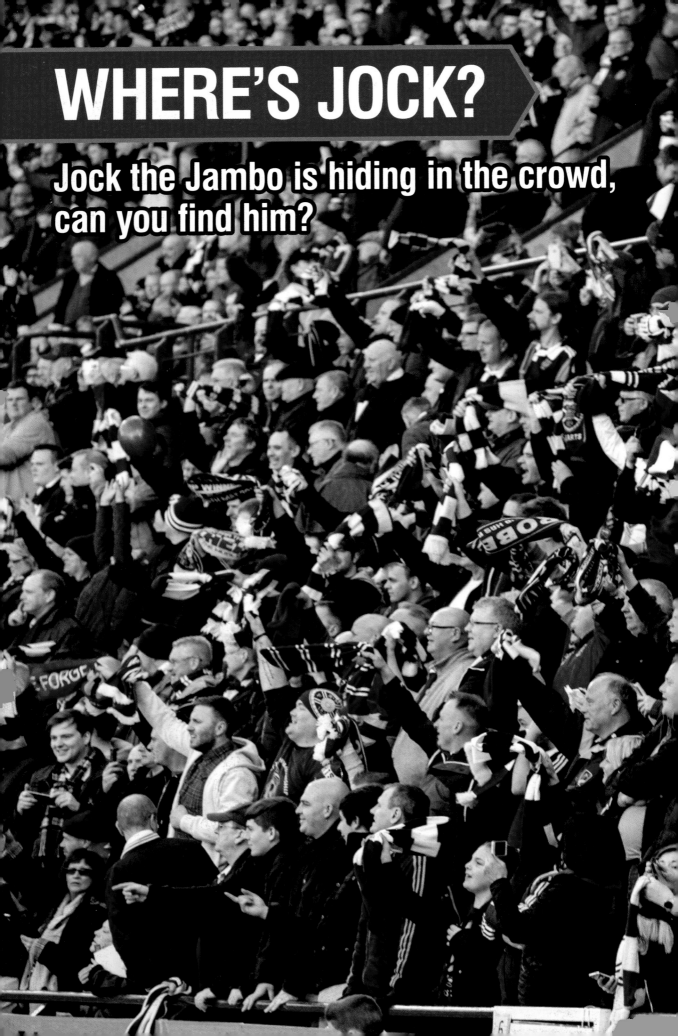

WHERE'S JOCK?

Jock the Jambo is hiding in the crowd, can you find him?